T0208203

MEGATON

E. A. DETLEFSEN

MEGATON

Copyright © 2020 E. A. Detlefsen.

All rights reserved. No part of this book may be used or reproduced by any means, graphic, electronic, or mechanical, including photocopying, recording, taping or by any information storage retrieval system without the written permission of the author except in the case of brief quotations embodied in critical articles and reviews.

This is a work of fiction. All of the characters, names, incidents, organizations, and dialogue in this novel are either the products of the author's imagination or are used fictitiously.

iUniverse books may be ordered through booksellers or by contacting:

iUniverse
1663 Liberty Drive
Bloomington, IN 47403
www.iuniverse.com
1-800-Authors (1-800-288-4677)

Because of the dynamic nature of the Internet, any web addresses or links contained in this book may have changed since publication and may no longer be valid. The views expressed in this work are solely those of the author and do not necessarily reflect the views of the publisher, and the publisher hereby disclaims any responsibility for them.

Any people depicted in stock imagery provided by Getty Images are models, and such images are being used for illustrative purposes only. Certain stock imagery © Getty Images.

ISBN: 978-1-5320-9241-1 (sc)
ISBN: 978-1-5320-9242-8 (e)

Library of Congress Control Number: 2020907923

Print information available on the last page.

iUniverse rev. date: 07/06/2020

Author's Prologue

N ature, for the most part, is dependable. It's a safe bet that summer follows spring, autumn follows summer, winter follows autumn, and spring follows winter. Hot expands and cold contracts. That's the dependable side of nature. However, sometimes nature has a hiccup, an oops. It throws us a curveball. There have been people born with six fingers for an example. My mother, her sister and her father could all hear a tune, sit down, and play it on the piano without ever having a single lesson. It's called playing by ear. I can't. My sisters can't. Back in 1918 in Alton, Illinois, a boy was born who grew to be 8 feet, 11 inches tall. His nickname was "The Alton Giant." It just goes to show you if the right chromosomes line up, extraordinary things can happen. So with that in mind, let me tell you a story about a very unusual, and wonderfully unique, giant horse.

Dedicated to John Byrd for showing me what
a powerful force imagination can be.

PART I

In rural America, near the end of summer, one of the best things happen… the County Fair. People from far and wide and from all four corners of the county come to see family and old friends. There are games to play, pie-eating contests, a Ferris wheel, and fireworks. Everything you need to have a good time is there. For some farm families, there is so much work to do around their farms it's the only time all summer they can see each other. They talk about the weather, discuss the work on the farm, and share their family news. They also come to see who has grown the best produce and made the best products. There are friendly competitions for the best corn, the best milk cow and the best rooster. And the women compete to see who brought the best pie crust, the best jams and jellies, and the best quilts.

One of the most popular contests at the fair is the heavy horse competition. These mild-mannered giants compete in games of agility and power. They drag dead weight to determine which horse is the strongest, and they run through obstacle courses to see how well the horses behave and listen to commands.

One year, an unusually large Shire stallion entered the contest. Shires are also known as "cold bloods" because of the colder climates of northern Europe from which they first came. This horse was one of the biggest the county had ever seen. It was twenty-one hands high, far taller than the average height of eighteen hands. His coloring was visually stunning with chestnut-colored hair in his mane and a tail as white as freshly fallen snow. His ancestors carried knights in armor back in England. His name was Thor after the Norse god of lightning and thunder.

Thor easily won the blue ribbon for being the strongest draft horse after dragging a sled of huge rocks farther and faster than any other in the competition.

In the equine pavilion across the aisle from Thor, there was a three-year-old Percheron filly owned by the La Beau family. She was nineteen hands high, slightly bigger than average. She was black as India ink. Her name was Coquette, a French name. Percherons came from the Perche region of France. Coquette won a blue ribbon for best of breed keeping alive a tradition the La Beau family and their lineage of Percherons had achieved for years. Her bloodline was known to go back many years back to 1806. Her great ancestors were coach horses for royal families in France.

As the day of friends and games came to a close and fireworks had ended, the music stopped, and the rides were shut down. The food venders sold the last of their popcorn, corn dogs, and funnel cakes and closed their trailers. The last of the animals were put up for the night and secured in their stalls, cages, and pens for the next day's events. After the crowd went home for the night, the fairgrounds grew silent and very tranquil. Nothing moved, not the animals, not the wind. It was very still for a good while.

Then it came. Slowly, the wind started blowing the light litter of paper cups and empty popcorn bags around the fairgrounds. It was a small rumbling at first. Then it grew louder. It seemed like heavy trucks on the nearby highway barreling in closer. Soon it sounded as if a train was rolling right down the center of the fairgrounds. The wind howled, whipped, and whirled, tearing the roofs off the buildings. Pavilions flew apart. Pigs, cows, horses, and other livestock ran for their lives. They ran and ran, not knowing where they were running. They just ran.

Early the next morning, those who had animals at the fair received the news of the tornado and what it had done. They came as fast as they could to see what damage had been done and couldn't believe what they saw. There were piles of lumber and sheet metal roofing where a pavilion once stood. To everyone's surprise, the duck and chicken pavilion had no damage at all. Tornados do funny things like that. Those who had livestock at the fair immediately started to look for their animals. They searched carefully, sorrowfully, hoping to find them well or learn the animals were able to run to safety. The search took days. Some lucky animals were discovered right away. Sadly, some were never found. Ben and Cora La Beau drove with the horse trailer in every direction from dawn to dusk for a week hoping Coquette was safe without success.

Two weeks had passed when a troop of hiking Boy Scouts that were earning their merit badges for compass reading found Coquette, Thor, and several of the missing horses. The displaced horses had instinctively gathered into a herd. The herd ran over six miles away from the fairgrounds and into a meadow where they felt safe hidden miles from the road. It was here the horses had found fresh meadow grass to eat and clean fresh stream water to drink. The Boy Scout troop returned with the news, and soon the horses' owners were called. It wasn't long before trailers arrived to drive off into different directions and return the horses to where they came from.

Eleven and one-half months later, during a lightning storm booming with thunder, a male foal was born to Coquette. Its body was black as night, like his mother. Its mane and tail were white, which in contrast to the black coat looked like lightning flashing. The only other spot that wasn't black was its white right front hoof.

That morning Dr. Otto Bodie, the veterinarian, was called to help with the foal and check out Coquette. Dr. Bodie was tall and lean, and even when he had a fresh haircut, he looked as though he still needed a haircut. He was the only veterinarian that Benedict La Beau had ever used. Dr. Bodie's father was the veterinarian for Ben's father. Dr. Bodie liked to come to the La Beau farm. He enjoyed seeing Vivian, Ben's sister, who always had fresh-baked treats. He also enjoyed visiting with Cora, Ben's daughter. Cora was always asking good questions, like "Why doesn't it hurt to nail shoes on a horse's hoof?"

"Their hooves are like your fingernails, Cora. When you do it right, they don't feel any different than when you trim your nails with a clipper," Dr. Bodie answered Cora. Cora loved learning as much as she could from Dr. Bodie.

"Coquette is our new prize winner, and this is her first foal. We want them both to be checked out," Ben instructed Dr. Bodie.

Ben had raised Coquette from a foal. He raised Percherons as did his father Maurice and his grandfather Claude La Beau three generations ago. Claude La Beau and his family brought their first Percherons into this country from France. Cora was also at the foaling. As an eleven-year-old growing up on a farm, this was not the first birth she had seen. In all, Cora witnessed the birth of five Percherons, nine chickens, one rooster (named Sun Rise) and a barn cat (referred to as "the cat"). The cat never wanted to be bothered, and the chickens didn't make good pets. Creatures that Cora thought made the best pets were horses and dogs. Of all the creatures on the farm, Cora liked the horses and a Golden Retriever named Sookie the best.

The horse barn had seven stalls. Four on one side and three on the other with an aisle down the middle. The side with three stalls had one which was twice the size of the others. That's where Coquette gave birth. The foal arrived without any problems or help.

"Look at the size of his cannon bones! I've never seen any like that before. They are exceptionally long," said Dr. Bodie.

Cannon bones are the bones between the carpel joint (the knee) and the fetlock joint (the ankle); they don't ever grow any longer after a horse is born. That's it, that's the size they will stay. That's why colts look long and lanky and out of proportion.

"This horse is going to be a giant!" Dr. Bodie exclaimed.

"We won't see it," Ben replied. "Someone else will feed and look after him. This half breed will be out of here as soon as he's old enough. We can't keep him here. He doesn't fit in with the rest." Ben felt that only purebloods should stay on the farm.

Cora didn't hear what was being said. She was falling in love with the new foal. He was wide-eyed and had a hard time standing up at first. He fell a few times, and this comedy just added to the feelings Cora was quickly developing for the newborn baby giant.

"Ben, look at Cora," Dr. Bodie said as he put his hand on Ben's shoulder. He liked to touch people when he felt he had something important to say.

"Are you seeing this, Ben? Just look at her."

Ben looked at his daughter. For the first time since her mother had died, Cora's eyes twinkled full and bright. She was smiling. She smiled before, but this time it was different. This time she was glowing. That funny-looking, legs-too-long, body-too-short, clumsy, baby-giant horse had lifted a sadness that had hung like a cloud over Cora for much too long. Ben smiled. He knew what was happening. He remembered the newborns when he was young, but this was different. Some mysterious connection between Cora and this foal was starting to take place.

"I'm glad I got to see this," said Dr. Bodie. "To see her smile like that makes the trip well worth it."

"I'm glad too. Cora has her mother's smile," admitted Ben.

No one talked about the foal anymore. Dr. Bodie walked to his van, and Ben walked with him. They shook hands, and soon Dr. Bodie drove off.

Ben's wife was named Elsa Andersen. She always claimed to be a relative of Hans Christian Andersen, the famous Danish storyteller, but never came up with any proof. She met Ben at the age of seventeen while at a farm auction with her father, Carl. Carl had a team of Belgians he kept as a hobby. While Maurice Le Beau and Carl Andersen were bidding against each other for the last of the hay wagons being auctioned off, Elsa and Ben talked of their horses. Ben told her about the Percherons, their history, and breeding them. Elsa told him about her family's Belgians and how, in the winter, they would hitch up the team to their sleigh and take family and friends for sleigh rides. She also told Ben how they'd put on snow skis and let one of the big Belgians pull them through the snow. As soon as Elsa was old enough, this was how she learned to ski. Many years later, Elsa taught Cora to ski like that too. It was an enjoyable thing for a mother and daughter to do on a winter's day out in the country. Coquettes' mother, Cozette, used to pull them through the snow for their ski outings. Cora picked it up right away. She learned quick and loved it.

Sookie came to live on the farm when Cora was about six years old, given to the La Beau's by the local butcher. The pup was bought and paid for before he was born. For some reason that no one knows he was never picked up. One day, about ten weeks after he was born and four weeks after he was to be taken home, all the rest of the litter had gone to their new homes, but one the puppy remained unclaimed. The butcher told Elsa the story and offered the puppy to her free of charge. Elsa took one look at the puppy. Knowing a bargain when she saw it, she brought him home to everyone's surprise. Elsa went to the butcher for beef and pork and came back with a puppy. Elsa did a lot of free-spirited things like that.

At ten weeks old, puppies get into everything as they explore and learn. One of the first things Sookie learned was that the cat had no use from him. It looked as if he tried to make friends with the cat, but the cat being older seemed to have no time for his playful, young energy. Sookie got his name after he discovered the fireplace. The fire was out, and he started to sniff around. When he came out, his face was full of soot, which made everyone laugh. Aunt Vivian laughed the most. She called him Soot Face, then Sootie, which eventually became Sookie. That was the version that stuck.

Cora and Sookie went to see the foal every morning while doing chores. They would go to the big stall and slowly move toward Coquette and the foul. Coquette knew that Cora was not going to harm her baby in any way, but she didn't like Sookie sniffing around. She would move in between her baby and Sookie and use her big head to push Sookie away.

Cora would start stroking Coquette, and when the foal felt that it was safe, he would move up to get stroked too. That's how it was for some time. When the foal was older, Cora and Sookie spent more time alone with the foal. Soon he was as tall as Cora already very strong. Cora could feel it.

Time passed, and the foal grew into a colt. Around the time it came to find a new home for the half breed, Ben saw the love and dedication Cora had shown the colt. He decided to keep it for Cora. It was a compassionate decision. The colt and Sookie became good friends and played together when Cora was at school. The colt was the only animal that had the energy to play with Sookie or even wanted too. Sookie would run between the colt's legs or run around him in circles. The colt would try to catch and nudge the dog with his head. They grew to be terrific friends.

Cora was smiling all the time now. She spent all her free time with the colt, and the two of them quickly developed a deep bond. He was learning trust, and she was feeling a sense of purpose. Cora was struggling to find just the right name for her colt. She thought of two French names. Jean La Hoof, a pun after the French pirate Jean La Fitte, because of the colt's one white hoof. The other option was Pied Blanc, French for White Foot. Neither name rang true for Cora.

While she kept them in mind, she didn't care for either of them.

One day while Cora was in science class, the lesson was about the nature of matter. She listened as her teacher, Mr. Allen Dial, spoke about atoms and their sub-atomic parts of neutrons, electrons, and protons. Mr. Dial taught two subjects like all the teachers at Cora's school. Mr. Dial taught science and math. He and his wife, Peggy, who felt she needed to escape her high-pressure job, moved from the city to live a quieter life in the country. When Allen heard about the teaching job in the country, he took it.

Mr. Dial was telling the class about the history of atomic power and how the nuclear bombs used in World War II had power that was measured in megatons. Cora's ears perked up, and her interest peaked. She raised her hand to ask a question.

"Yes, Cora?" asked Mr. Dial.

"What is a megaton?" inquired Cora.

"Good question, Cora," he replied. "One megaton is the explosive power of one million tons of TNT."

She knew right then and there as soon as she knew the meaning of the word.

"That's it! A perfect fit," she thought.

That day the bus ride home seemed to last much longer than usual. Cora was happy, excited, and eager to share the name that came to her as if she was struck by lightning herself. Her unnamed powerful baby giant horse was now Megaton.

PART II

Two years passed, and Cora was almost thirteen. Megaton had grown too. He had really grown. He stood twenty-eight hands high at the withers and weighed close to three thousand pounds.

Cora worked with him every day after school. On the weekends, she would work him in the morning and take long rides in the afternoon. Megaton was eager and willing to learn, and he learned fast. During the winter, they worked on skiing and learning voice commands. "HEE" was the command for a right turn, and "HAW" was the command for a left turn. This was very helpful for skiing behind him.

He was also taught to take riders on his back. His girth made it hard for people to sit on his back. To ride horseback style on Megaton, a specialized saddle was made by the local leather smith, Wally Carlson. The saddle was a combination of Western and English style saddles. It was a wide strap of leather twenty inches wide with a thick rope and knot instead of a saddle horn. It had three stirrups in total, two stirrups on the left side and only one on the right. The two on the left were there so anyone could climb up like a stepladder. You would start by grabbing the saddle horn rope, then put your right foot in the lower stirrup followed by your left foot into the top stirrup and finally swing your right leg over and sit flat on the saddle. His headgear was distinctive too. Wally made a large bridle for his big head with a noseband, browband, throatlatch, headpiece, and reins. Cora didn't want it to have a bit. Megaton learned just fine without it.

The La Beau farm was a working farm. Like all farms, everyone and everything worked. They all had a part to play. Ben planted, cut, and bailed hay. Aunt Vivian, Ben's older sister, kept the house and cooked. She was born with diminished mental capabilities. They say she didn't get enough oxygen when she was a baby. She hardly ever left the farm, and she never had a social life. Cora tended the chickens, collected the eggs, and took care of the horses. The chickens ate bugs and laid eggs. The barn cat caught mice. Sookie barked when someone would come up the driveway and kept the big varmints away. Megaton being a half breed, was not breeding stock, so he pulled hay wagons and moved heavy things around the farm. If the truth were said, he was really there for Cora. They didn't need him to pull hay wagons. They had a tractor for that, but it was a useful skill for a horse of his size to learn. He had his pulling gear made just for him crafted once again by Wally Carlson. The pulling equipment was a three-inch-wide breast collar with sheep's hide on the inside as a cushion. One of the straps went up and over his shoulders and the other across his chest parallel to the ground attached with two steel rings on both sides for hooking up chains for pulling. The command "PULL" was used when Megaton needed to start moving forward. If the load was massive, "TUG" was used, and Megaton would put in the extra needed effort.

One day after an extraordinarily heavy rain, a low spot deep in the hayfield became saturated and marshy. The tractor got stuck in mud up to its axle. Even with all its power and four-wheel drive, the wheels had no traction and just whirled around like pinwheels. After sizing up the situation, Ben had an idea and walked back to the house to get help from Megaton.

"Cora, get Megaton. He's got a job to do. Let's see what your giant can do." Ben told her. Back where the tractor was stuck, they put the pulling harness on Megaton. They hooked him up to the front of the tractor. Cora patted Megaton on the chest.

"Pull, Megaton, PULL," she said, and Megaton started forward. The slack came out of the chains, but the tractor didn't budge.

"PULL," she yelled again. Nothing happened. Cora patted Megaton on the neck.

"TUG, Megaton TUG," she cheered him on. Megaton didn't want to disappoint her. He reached forward with his one white hoof and tugged. Shifting all of his massive body weight forward, the chain became taut. No slack was left. Megaton took a step forward with his back hooves. His front hooves raised into the air as his rear hooves dug in, and he leaned forward again. The tractor also moved... just a bit, but enough for Megaton to get all four of his hooves flat on the ground. With all four hooves flat on the ground, Megaton tugged and pulled. In hardly any time at all, the tractor was free and ready to roll. After the tractor was free of the mud, Ben noticed something that simultaneously shocked and embarrassed him.

"That's an exceptional horse you have there. Would you believe I forgot and left the tractor in gear? That must have been like pulling ten tractors for him."

Cora was pleased to hear it. Megaton sensed the pride that Cora felt and knew he had pleased her. He liked that feeling.

"Megaton will win every event at the County Fair this year. I just know it," she told Ben excitedly.

"Cora," Ben looked at her eye-to-eye and replied sadly, "Oh sweetheart, Megaton is a half breed. He will never compete at the Fair."

PART

III

Saturdays were the days for riding. Megaton and Cora would ride for hours along the roadside or make trails of their own. Wherever they meandered to, they always made it a point to visit Wadlow Park. Wadlow Park was a large park with a sledding hill, swings for the younger kids, and a gazebo bandshell seldom used except for the Fourth of July or weddings.

Megaton liked being at the park, and all of the kids loved seeing and petting the giant horse. Some would bring apples and carrots for a snack. Megaton loved the attention. They would spend a few hours in the park, and it would be time to go. On horseback, it took a good while to get back to the farm.

One day when the duo left the park, Cora decided to stay on the main road so the trip home would be faster. Megaton clomped along with a rhythm like an old faithful grandfather clock. The town was to their backs, and the country road lay ahead with overhanging trees and the sun far past midway in the sky. Clomp, clomp, clomp. The sound of Megaton's heavy hooves was the only sound to be heard.

The road sloped into a shallow valley, which at one time had a river that ran through it. Only run-off rainwater from the higher ground came through a large culvert under the road now. It provided just enough water to maintain a swamp on the lower side of the road. The swamp was an ideal environment for cattails and canary grass.

When Megaton reached the crest of the valley, Cora looked down and saw skid marks that ran off the road into the swamp. When they got down to the skid marks, they saw the tire tracks leading right into a trail of crushed cattails and canary grass. As they got even closer, they heard a baby crying.

A mother and child going to town driving a small hardtop sports car had run off the road. As it turned out, a deer came out of the swamp just as the vehicle went over the ridge. The mother swerved not to hit it, slid off the road, and went into the swamp. Water and mud prevented the doors from opening. The front wheels and hood were well underwater, and being a hardtop, the mother and child couldn't get out.

Cora told Megaton, "We've got to help them." They trudged through the mud to see what could be done.

"Are you alright?" Cora called out.

The baby was scared and crying very loud. The mother yelled over the crying.

"MY BABY, HELP MY BABY, HELP MY BABY!" She was thinking only of her baby before herself. Cora didn't know if she should ride and get help or think of some way to help them. She knew that Megaton could easily pull the little car out of the swamp. Cora dismounted and, while up to her knees in swamp water, took the rope off of Megaton's custom saddle. She tied it to the lower stirrup on the left side of the custom saddle that had two stirrups for extra length.

She then tied the other end to the little car's bumper and gave the rig a jerk. It felt like it would do the job.

Cora climbed up on to Megatons back and started to give him voice commands. The baby was still screaming. The mother, not knowing what was going on in the back of the car, began to panic.

"GET HELP! GO, GET HELP!" she pleaded.

Cora gave the command to TUG. She didn't bother with PULL. He knew something was expected of him, and he would do it. He pulled his hooves up and out of the mud and stepped backward. With each step he took, his hooves sank in the mud. It was not easy for him to walk in the mud backward. He had to lift his hooves up higher than usual, and his weight didn't help. Because of that, even pulling that little car was hard work. Megaton had the muscle and the heart. It was his coordination through the mud that gave him the most trouble. Cora kept cheering him on, and soon the little car was free of the mud and water. The doors were able to be opened, the frightened baby and the mother were able to get out the car and step on the semi-solid ground.

The mother was Rose Staily, wife of Rodger Staily, who was the president of the chamber of commerce and the son of the town president Ike Staily. Her baby's name was Rodger Jr. When Rose set foot on the semi-solid ground again with her baby in her arms, she couldn't believe her eyes. Amid her panic, she was unclear what happened outside of the car. Now, she started to understand what had, in fact, occurred. A young girl and a giant horse had pulled them to safety and got them out of the swamp.

Cora introduced herself and Megaton.

"Thank you. Your timing was perfect. Thank you for being here," said Rose.

"Thank Megaton," Cora replied, "He did all the work."

"Thank you, big fellow," Rose said as she patted him on the nose.

Megaton knew he had done something right, and he felt pride in what he had done. The car could not be driven.

"We'll ride you back to town, and you can call your family," Cora said. Cora, Rose, and Roger Jr. got up on Megaton's back and headed back to town.

"What a handsome horse you have here," said Rose.

"We almost didn't keep him," Cora said. Then she told Rose the story of how Megaton came to be her horse. She explained the history of how her whole family raised Percherons, the tornado, and how Coquette was lost.

"Well, I, for one, am glad that Megaton is still around," replied Rose. All the way home, Cora praised Megaton for the job he did.

By the time Cora got back to the farm, it was hours past the time she said she'd be back, and the sun was about to set. As they rode up the long driveway, Sookie was barking. They saw Ben standing at the top of the driveway.

"We are sooo late, Megaton. This doesn't look good," Cora said to Megaton.

Ben stood fast in the driveway with his arms folded as they rode up to him. Cora held back on the reins to slow the pace. The closer they got, the slower they moved, thinking a scolding was on the way. Ben took hold of the reigns.

"You're late," he said.

Cora was about to tell him the story.

"I'm so proud of the two of you!" he surprised them by not being angry. "Everyone in town has been calling. You two heroes are big news. The town president called. He wanted to thank you personally for what you did for his family. The newspaper called too. They want an interview and pictures of the local heroes. News travels faster than you would think in a country town."

The next day Megaton was out in his own coral, separate from the pure-blooded Percherons. Ben, Cora, and Vivian went to church like they did every Sunday. The whole Staily family was there, including Big Rodger, Rose, Baby Rodger, and Ike Staily. That Sunday, the Reverend Dr. Dennis Fischer gave a sermon about stepping up to help, how easy it is and that even a kid and a giant horse could do it. He told the story of David and Goliath. He reminded the congregation that no matter how great the odds, just try, have faith, and in the end, you may surprise yourself.

Dr. Fischer had been the reverend for twenty-five years. He baptized, married, and buried a lot of people over that time. He knew the La Beau family well as they were always avid churchgoers and even buried Cora's mother. As a silver anniversary gift for his years of service to the church, the congregation pitched in and raised money to buy a new bell for the bell tower in his name. The old bell wasn't that old. It was electric, but no one really liked the sound it made.

On the way out of the church, everyone saw the La Beaus and wanted to know how Megaton was doing. Dr. Bodie was there too.

"From the moment I set eyes on that colt, I knew special things were in store. I could easily see this giant was no ordinary horse," he said.

After church, as people were leaving, Rose and her family walked up to Cora and her family. Rose had brought a basket of apples, carrots, and celery for Megaton.

"Be sure my giant hero gets this," she said.

"I will make sure he does, and thank you," Cora replied.

Ike Staily told Cora that he had arranged time with the local newspapers to take pictures next Wednesday evening at Wadlow Park. They all agreed to the plan, and Cora felt proud in anticipation.

Cora didn't go to school on Wednesday. Ben was okay with it. She did her chores and then ran to Megaton's stall. First, she hosed him down and brushed him. Megaton liked the hose. To him, it felt like a deep muscle massage, and the brushing was relaxing, like a day at a spa for the big hero. His mane and tail were clean and bright white. His black coat shined like a new pair of patent leather shoes. Soon it was time to head to town for the pictures.

For this special occasion, Megaton was driven to town in the horse trailer. This kept him clean, and it was also much faster. When they pulled up to Wadlow Park, almost everyone was there. Megaton was backed out of the horse trailer. When the crowd cheered at the sight of him, he felt their excitement and liked it. He looked buffed and polished and ready for anything.

Megaton behaved like a true hero, quiet and unaffected, while cameras clicked, and lights flashed. The gentle giant just stood still and waited for Cora's directions. Reporters took pictures in every combination. Megaton and Cora, Megaton and Rose, Megaton, Cora, Rose, and baby Rodger and even one of baby Rodger sitting on Megaton that made the horse look even more massive and baby Rodger tiny. Even Ike Staily had his picture taken with Megaton. It was news, and being the town president, he just wanted one for his office wall.

The reporters asked lots of questions. Most of them were stupid like "How did you feel at the time?" and "What were you thinking?" One question, however, Cora thought was particularly ignorant. A tall, all too skinny reporter in a tan trench coat asked Cora if she had any doubt that Megaton could do the job.

19

"Megaton has always done whatever I ask of him. He has never let me down," she replied. "And that car is so small I knew he could do it!"

Everybody secretly hoped for a ride on Megaton. However, no one got a ride that day. Kids, teenagers, and the grownups just patted and stroked him while marveling at the size and good nature of the giant.

After the photos were taken and the crowd thinned out, and it was time to go home. It was back into the horse trailer for Megaton. On the way home, Ben and Cora talked about what a special horse Megaton was and how happy they were that they decided to let him stay.

PART

IV

Dr. Fischer waited outside the church. It was a bright and warm Friday, and the church's new bell was on its way. As he looked at his pocket watch, he became worried because the delivery was late, and he had somewhere to be. Friday night was Bingo night, and he oversaw the group of teenagers that set up tables and chairs in the Bingo room. The delivery truck took the highway, and even though it moved faster, it was the long way to get to the road that led to the church.

Just when Dr. Fischer was about to ask his wife Paula to wait for the truck in his place, it pulled up. It was a six-wheel flatbed with a crane to do the lifting. The only cargo on the flatbed was the bell, which was protected by a four-post wooden crate and heavy plastic. Dr. Fischer decided to stay and take care of business.

The driver hopped out of the cab and climbed up on the flatbed to operate the crane. He attached the hook to the wooden crate and started the crane.

"That's one big, heavy bell," the driver said. The bell was lifted off the flatbed and swung in the direction of the churchyard. Finally, it was lowered to the ground with a dull thud. Dr. Fischer thanked the driver and signed the receiving bill. Having completed what needed to be done, both men drove off in opposite directions to take care of what was next for them.

The old electric bell (which was just four large speakers pointing in each direction) had been disconnected and removed earlier. The old bell rope and axel were still in place from when the church was built. A pulley and cable were installed outside the bell tower so the new bell could be lifted up and into the bell tower. The plan was to install it on Saturday so that the new bell could toll for all to enjoy Sunday morning.

Saturday, just before noon, the volunteers started to assemble ready to work installing the new bell. The women brought Jell-O molds and homemade cookies. Mr. Dial got the plan going with the science and engineering of it. He planned to hoist the bell up to the bell tower with a machine called a ladder-vader, which was a combination ladder and elevator. Roofers use such a contraption to get bundles of shingles up on to a roof using a small gas-powered engine with a cable and belt. When the lever on the belt was pulled tight, the wire coiled up, and the platform raises the ladder. Releasing the lever lets gravity bring the platform back down.

All was set, and the new bell would soon be at the top of the bell tower, so everyone thought. First off, the bell was set too far from the steeple and in too narrow of a space. The new bell sitting square on the ground was too heavy to be moved by the work party. Someone had the idea to drag the bell by hooking the cable of the ladder-vader to the bell crate. The small engine was started, the cable was attached to the bell crate, and the lever was pulled. The slack slowly came out of the cable. The wooden box began to move, but not forward. The top of the crate tilted towards the gas engine, but the bottom stood still. Before it could be stopped, the container was on its side, and the small gas engine fell over breaking off the gas tank, and the engine stopped instantly. Without a gas tank, the engine would not start again. Mr. Dial and the work party looked at one another and shook their heads in disbelief.

"Oh no," someone murmured.

"What do we do now?" someone asked.

"Don't lose faith," said Dr. Fischer. "It's not over. We can do this! We will find a way."

Like every Saturday, Megaton was on his way to Wadlow Park enjoying the attention he got. Why Cora and Megaton chose to go past the church that day on their way to Wadlow Park, no one can say. They didn't go that way any other time. Maybe they wanted to witness the work being done, or perhaps fate led them there.

Clomp, clomp, clomp, clomp. The sound of Megaton's heavy hooves was approaching up the street.

"HERES OUR HORSEPOWER!" somebody yelled as Megaton got closer to the church.

"Megaton can do it," another person said.

When Cora and Megaton arrived at the church, Dr. Fischer ran to ask Cora if she would please have Megaton help get the bell into the steeple.

"Megaton would be happy to," she replied.

Mr. Dial found a piece of sheet metal to act as a sled and put it next to the bell crate. Once the bell was upright again, it would set on the sheet metal to reduce friction. Then Megaton could drag the bell crate across the grass to where it needed to be. Megaton had the bell crate upright on the sled in no time. The bell was soon dragged across the lawn to the base of the bell tower as easy as a kid would pull a wagon. The bell was in place and ready to be hoisted up to the bell tower. Everyone at the church was prepared to do their part, whatever that part was, as soon as they were needed.

Megaton was the leading player now. All eyes were on him. Everyone wanted to witness this beautiful, gentle, and willing mass of muscle in action. Mr. Dial checked all the riggings, ropes, and pulleys. Megaton was in place, and the work began. The two of them working as one was like watching a well-choreographed dance with Cora leading with voice commands and Megaton confidently following her lead. The crowd grew silent as this ballet took place with everyone watching every move they made.

The bell began to rise off the ground. Higher and higher it went. Megaton just took one step after another as if it were one of his Saturday strolls. Soon the new bell was up to the top of the steeple. It was swung into the bell tower by the work party, and the onlookers cheered.

"Good job, Megaton, and Cora!" the work party applauded and praised them. Cora was proud of him, and he was glad to please her. With the work done, everyone went for cookies, Jell-O, and cold drinks.

"How divine it was that you and Megaton showed up," Dr. Fischer said in awe of what took place. "It was a beautiful thing to see. That horse is a wonderful animal. The love you two show each other is inspiring and something everyone can learn from."

Mr. Dial went to thank Cora and Megaton.

"Thank you both. We were lost without your help," Mr. Dial said. "You know, Cora, I believe that horse would do anything, I mean anything, you asked of him."

Cora just smiled and gave Megaton a big hug around his big neck. She took a few cookies for the ride home.

The word of Megaton spread to other towns around the county. Megaton was news now and the talk of the county. Not only did his name become known, but the stories grew. Soon he was known to be the biggest horse ever known around this part of the county, and it wasn't just a small car he pulled out of the swamp. The story turned into a busload of kids. The new church bell had grown to weigh multiple tons, and it was nothing less than a church miracle that Megaton performed.

The stories of Megaton triggered the memories of a group of old farmers as they sat in barbershops and at coffee houses. They talked to each other about the horse and wagon days and told yarns of amazing things horses have done. Most of the stories were tall tales or hearsay. Some of the stories went on and on, and each one more fantastic than the other.

Megaton was stirring both the memory and the imagination of the entire county. He gave the community a sense of renewed pride as if he were a famous hometown quarterback, major league pitcher, or Olympic gold medal champion. People from other towns wanted to see the "Super Horse" to decide for themselves if what all the talk was about was real. Calls were made to the La Beau farm asking about Megaton. One wise guy called asking to talk to Megaton. Ben didn't like those calls coming to the house. The phone was a tool for communicating, not a toy. He had no tolerance for that kind of nonsense.

The local radio station got into the act too with made up Megaton sightings. One caller said, "I saw Megaton at Ernie's Bar. The bartender asked, 'Hey Megaton, why the long face?'" Soon the radio disc jockey was asking for more horse stories, which led to more horse jokes and other made up Megaton sightings that were phoned in regularly.

One day a call came in to the radio station.

"I knew of a horse that will make Megaton look like an old broodmare. Compared to this horse I saw, Megaton's a washed–up, retired racehorse," the caller said.

"Okay, caller. Tell us about this horse you have," the D.J. encouraged.

"I don't own the horse. But I know a guy who knows the owner," the caller defended.

"So, this horse your friend knows about is more horse than Megaton?" the D.J. asked, smelling a good publicity stunt a mile away. After hearing news of this horse who could challenge the legend, he couldn't resist and quickly threw down the gantlet. "We found a contender. Come out, come out where ever you are, Megaton? Let's see just what you can do!"

The D.J.'s name was Sandy Metek. He gave up working overnights at a city radio station where his radio name was Sandy, the Sandman, Metek. He took up the name Sandman because of the overnight shift, not because he was boring. He heard about a daytime job in the country and, since he was ready for a change, took the job. Metek being new to the area and Megaton's growing fame was a perfect fit. He wanted to really play it up big. The publicity could only help his career.

"Tell me, caller, can we get these two horses together?" asked Metek.

"I'll try if you keep talking about it on the air. My friend's friend will surely hear it, and the chances will be much better," the caller plotted.

All of Cora's classmates listened to Metek in the Morning. He was the new thing and the young listeners like him. That's when the questions started.

"Can Megaton beat the other horse?" and "Is Megaton going to meet this challenge?" they would ask. Cora didn't care one way or the other. She loved Megaton, and a contest between the two horses would be just a waste of time and effort. It wouldn't prove anything, she thought.

Metek called the La Beau farm one morning, and Ben answered the phone. Metek didn't know any of the facts, but that didn't stop him from asking Ben why he was afraid of bringing Megaton to this challenge. Ben didn't have time for this and said Megaton was his daughters' horse. He told Metek that she alone decided what Megaton will or won't do.

"Can you call her to the phone?" asked Metek. Ben looked at the time and said.

"No. She's leaving for school!" Ben said sternly.

"But… Can…" That was all Metek could to say before Ben hung up the phone.

"Looks like someone is running scared," Metek said over the air so all could hear it.

When Cora got to school, everyone was thinking the same thing. Several kids called out, "Are you afraid? What's the matter? Scared? The great Megaton can't do it? No show La Beau." The kids she thought were her friends and who had ridden Megaton at Wadlow Park were suddenly taunting her. Cora couldn't believe what was happening.

To add to the mix, the other horse had been found and was ready to meet Megaton.

"Anytime, anywhere," reported Metek over the radio.

Mr. Dial stopped Cora between classes.

"Are you doing okay, Cora? Megaton is quite the topic, and I know about the teasing around school."

"I don't know," Cora said. "Why is this happening? Can't we just be left alone?" Cora questioned.

"It's a tough spot you're in. What are you going to do?" Mr. Dial asked.

"I don't know," Cora replied. "All the kids are teasing me and think maybe Megaton can't do it. Megaton has never done anything like this before. He has never competed."

"What is the harm in accepting this challenge?" Mr. Dial asked. "From what I've seen of Megaton, I believe he would do very well."

"It's my part in all of this. I don't know if I'll do well. What if I fail? Then everyone will blame Megaton. It's a big decision, and I don't know what to do," Cora answered.

After school, when Cora got home, the phone rang. It was Ike Staily. He heard about Metek's challenge. He wanted to hold the contest in town at Wadlow Park to set up the home field advantage and let everyone in town root for Megaton.

Cora was now more confused than ever, and the pressure was mounting. She wished she had her mother to ask about this. Her mother was good at helping her with decisions. Feeling no one could possibly understand, and without her mother to talk to, she felt very alone. She could try to talk to Ben about it, but she feared he wouldn't understand. She wanted to talk to a woman who would understand the social pressures a teenage girl feels at school. Aunt Vivian was always kind, but Cora felt she wouldn't understand the demands of being a reluctant celebrity.

A few days later, Cora walked across the school parking lot to the bus stop when Rose Staily drove up. The Chamber of Commerce had recently held a book drive, and Rose was delivering the books she collected for the school in her new car.

"Hey, Cora!" Rose called out. "Look at my new car. I hear that my hero is famous. It's all over the radio. Sounds like Megaton could run for public office," Rose said.

"That's all I need… more pressure," Cora replied as she started to cry.

"Cora, what's wrong? What do you mean?" Rose asked.

"The kids at school are teasing me about Megaton. They say he's not up for the challenge. I'm the one who hears it. I'm in the middle, the spotlight. I'm getting the pressure. My mom would know just what to do. I miss my mom," answered Cora trying to hold back sniffles. "Do I put him on display? Maybe get him hurt? Do I accept the challenge to stop this teasing, or do I really want Megaton to show everyone that he is the best horse ever?" she said no longer able to hold back tears. "I miss my mom. She could help."

Cora started to cry even harder. Rose remembered what it felt like to be a teenage girl at Cora's age and gave her a big hug.

"There is nothing wrong with doing it for both reasons, Cora. Do it to stop the teasing and do it to show off your wonderful horse. It's okay to do that. It's alright to show off sometimes. With a partner like Megaton, it's a perfect combination to let your light shine," Rose answered inspiritingly.

Cora felt better after hearing this from Rose but still far from sure about what to do when she got home. Cora walked right out to the barn, sat down, and talked to Megaton.

"What should we do, Megaton? Do we want to do this stupid competition? Since they won't let you compete at the county fair, this could your big chance. I know you can do it. If we do this, we can show them. We can show them all." Her confidence was building.

Megaton seemed to know what Cora wanted from him. As Cora looked into Megaton's eyes, they seem to say, "Okay, let's do it." She jumped up, gave him a big hug around his neck, and smiled.

"Let's go win!" she said.

Cora sprinted back to the house to tell Ben her decision.

"Is that your decision?" Ben asked, surprised. "Well, we better get started on his training if we're going to win," Ben said.

The next day at school, Cora told everyone that Megaton was going to meet the challenge and that they should spread the word. She knew she needed to call Ike Staily and let him know Megaton would accept the challenge and would win it. Just as Cora predicted, the word went around just as fast as any phone call. The next morning, Metek was all over it.

"I've done it. I've set it up," Metek enthusiastically called out, taking full credit for all of it. He called the La Beau house, and this time Cora answered. She was listening to the radio and was expecting his call.

"We are on the air with Megaton's owner Miss Cora La Beau," Metek reported. The fast-talking D.J. didn't give Cora much of a chance to talk. All Cora could tell him is that Mr. Ike Staily, the town president, offered to host it in Wadlow Park.

"I can't talk anymore. The bus will be here soon. Bye," Cora abruptly said and hung up the phone.

A few bus stops later, kids who heard Cora on the air started to get on the bus. They were talking about the radio interview.

"Metek didn't give you much chance to talk," one kid said.

"That was cool to hear someone I know live on the air," another one said.

The attention started to feel good, and Cora liked the feeling. A short while ago she was being teased, and now she was the center of good attention.

A call came to the house later that same evening. It was Big Roger, president of the Chamber of Commerce. He told Cora that he was happy she accepted, and he would do all the work of setting it up.

"I'll make all the calls and prepare the arrangements. And tomorrow, I'll call Metek in the Morning, so keep your radio on. You'll have to tell me all you can about Megaton, I need to do a lot of publicity," he told Cora.

She agreed, and they set up a meeting for the next Saturday.

Big Rodger was no stranger to pomp and circumstance and was a bit of a showman himself. When he was young, while most boys his age were out catching frogs, toads, and shooting tin cans with slingshots, he was home practicing to be a ventriloquist. He produced a verity show at the local high school just so he could be on stage. In college, his major was business with a minor in theater. He was always eager and ready to put on a show.

The next morning the call from Big Rodger came on

the radio just as planned. Metek put the call on the air right away when he found out it was regarding Megaton.

"You're on the air, caller," Metek said.

"This is Roger Staily. I'm Megaton's agent," Big Rodger told him.

"Agent? AGENT? Megaton has an agent now," Metek exclaimed.

"Well, you do know Megaton is a horse, right? He can't speak for himself. He's not Mr. Ed, you know," Big Rodger explained.

Metek told Big Rodger that he'd be the agent of the other horse. Big Rodger replied, "If you're his agent, then I guess we'll be doing some business together." Soon the jokes turned to insults as both men sensed this would be good for the event's PR.

"When we're done, Megaton will be dog food," Metek spouted.

"Have you ever even seen the other horse?" Big Rodger asked. The barbs went back and forth, and soon it was time to quit talking. Metek went to a commercial, but not before Big Rodger in true show business style announced the time and place.

The very next Saturday, Cora and Big Rodger met at the Le Beau farm to discuss everything about Megaton. They walked out to Megaton's private coral.

"He's huge!" exclaimed Big Rodger when he saw Megaton. He wasn't at Wadlow Park on day Megaton's pictures were taken for the newspapers. This was actually the first he ever saw Megaton.

Cora told Big Roger all about Megaton's history.

"Publicity is going to be easy with an origin story like Megaton. The truth is all we will need. We couldn't write it better if we tried."

Big Roger had set up the contest to be held during the town's annual scarecrow festival. The scarecrow festival brought a lot of people to town. It was big business for the shops, merchants, and street vendors. Big Roger was counting on Megaton's challenge adding a whole new element to the event. He even called a printer in town and created posters that were put on every lamppost and store.

MEGATON AT WADLOW PARK
Come One, Come All
See Megaton, our local favorite in a
display of power, and courage!
Music will be provided by *UNITED
CORN* in the festival bandshell
1:00 P.M.

The whole town was behind Megaton. Calls of support came to the La Beau house. Farmers were offering tons of free oats for Megaton to give him strength. The school had given Cora a pass on homework so she could keep training Megaton. UNITED CORN even wrote a song just for Megaton.

UNITED CORN was a strange group. The lead singer could only sing in the key of C and played the harmonica. There was a clarinet player, an accordion player, one guitar player that only played rhythm, a standup bass player, and a drummer. No one knew how the band did it, but they managed to make it work. People liked them, and they managed to book a lot of gigs. They even played at the County Fair years ago the night of the tornado.

Megaton worked very hard to train. Cora put in a lot of hours, as did Ben. With all the work needed to be done on the farm, Ben and Cora had few projects together. This one, however, was a lot of fun for both of them and allowed them to work closely together. Ben let Cora run the training while he helped get the dead weight drag working. Ben sat in the tractor with the brake on, and Megaton pulled it. The three of them felt just by working together, and the fun they had doing it was itself a personal victory. Cora enjoyed preparing so much that she felt, in a sense, they had already won the challenge.

Soon, the town had put the final touches on the Scarecrow fest. Every storefront down Main Street had its own scarecrow it had sponsored sitting in various poses. The scarecrows ranged from pumpkin-headed monsters to ballerinas and everything in-between, but mostly they were puns. The Scarecrow Fest let the town's residents and visitors vote on which scarecrow best fit the name it was given and the quality of construction. Last year's winner was a trash can with Tartan fabric made to look like a Scottish kilt, two ping-pong paddles as pectoral fins, a stovepipe neck, a kettle gourd for a head, and two ping pong balls as eyes giving it the appearance of a lizard's head. It was named "The Schlock Mess Monster."

Two sets of bleachers were rented and set up at the foot of the bandshell in Wadlow Park, creating an arena in the center. One set of bleachers was set up on the north side of the field and one set on the south side with the bandshell to the east. The bandshell was actually just a six-sided gazebo with three removable sides. It was built on the east side of the park so that audiences wouldn't be looking towards the setting sun in the West during evening activities. This forward-thinking design consideration was lost on most of the town since the bandshell was hardly ever used. Since Megaton's challenge was at one o'clock, the sun would be nearly overhead again. The strategic insight of the park's designer went without notice once again. Big Roger was running around, inspecting, and checking all the details. He was pleased with the way things were going.

"Metek in the Morning," the radio screeched. "It won't be long until the big day, folks. Give me a call and cast your vote. Megaton or my horse, Jumbo Jim? If you can't make it to Wadlow Park for our live remote radio broadcast and the annual scarecrow fest tune in and get all the details as they happen. I'll be on the air live, so come on out if you can and say hi".

Metek had gone to a commercial when the phone rang. It was Big Rodger, and he had a few things to say about the event. He was plugging the whole fest, not just the horse contest.

"We're back," Metek said. "And we have Rodger Staily on the air." Metek in true D.J. fashion started taunting right away. "Megaton is going down," he barked. "Jumbo Jim is going to win and win big!"

"Have you ever seen this other horse yet?" asked Big Rodger.

"I have all I need to know," answered Metek. "But what can you give us as far details go about this embarrassment Megaton is going to face, Roger?"

"Megaton and this great mystery horse you claim is so wonderful will meet in competition starting at one o'clock at Wadlow Park. That's one week from this coming Saturday," Big Rodger replied. "Get there early and enjoy the shops, and vote on your favorite scarecrow."

"What do you have planned for the contest?" asked Metek.

"It will be the best of three events," Big Rodger answered. "We have an obstacle course that requires saddle riding, a dead weight pull to see which horse is the strongest and one more thing you may want to get your horse to practice... responding to voice commands. Can your horse do that? Oh, I forgot, you don't know what this horse can do because you have never seen him. Or is it a her? Do you even know?" Big Roger continued to heckle the D.J. He made it a point to be sure and never mention the other horse by name. Big Roger knew marketing, and there was no benefit in having any other name other than Megaton ring out over the airwaves.

"What if it is a her. Is Megaton afraid of losing to a girl?" Metek replied.

"I must say," Big Rodger told Metek. "For an agent who is so uninformed about his client, you sure stick to your story. We'll see you in Wadlow Park."

"I believe my listeners, and if they say Jumbo Jim is better. I'm sticking with them." Then Metek broke away from his broadcast to go to the news.

Megaton worked hard every day. The trio of Megaton, Cora, and Ben had fun with the routine of Megaton's training, which made him look like a chiseled onyx statue of a champion. The time had come, and Megaton was ready.

On Friday morning, Metek filled up his entire show talking about the competition and remained steadfast in his position of just how bad Megaton was going to lose. Cora heard the Metek show while eating breakfast and kept quiet. She had never done anything like this before, and a ball of stage fright was building in her stomach. At school, her classmates wished Megaton good luck.

"Cora, you know there will be hundreds of people watching tomorrow? Do a good job," a random classmate called down the hall. There were other similar well wishes, none of which helped Cora's nerves.

By Friday afternoon, the students were eager to be

dismissed. The atmosphere was light and smooth, almost like free-time without the chaos. Everyone was excited for the next day ahead and the events at Wadlow Park. Everything was ready and in place. Big Rodger was already out on Main Street talking with vendors and shop owners.

On Saturday morning the town was like a beehive. The action started early, and the street vendors were poised to sell their arts and crafts. There were vendors selling flea market items, candles, earrings, and hot deep-fried snacks. The shop owners propped up their scarecrows one last time opened their storefronts, and made sure that everyone who came into their stores received a ballet for the scarecrow vote. The parking lot at Wadlow Park looked like a patchwork quilt with cars and trucks of every make and color. Big Rodger had covered everything. There were even designated parking spaces on each end of the bleachers for Megaton and Jumbo Jim. Each spot was big enough for a truck and a horse trailer and marked with a sign large enough that nobody could possibly miss them. Two gas generators to power the public address system at the bandshell were started, and the system was tested.

"Testing… testing, one, two, one, two," Big Rodger spoke into the microphone. "Can you hear me, Rodger?" as he waved to Rose and Baby Rodger, who were at the other end of the arena. Rose picked up Baby Rodger out of the stroller and told Baby Rodger to wave to his daddy. They both waved back to Big Rodger.

Metek heard the system test and walked up to the bandshell. He asked around to learn which of the men around the arena was Rodger Staley. Big Rodger heard him asking, walked up to Metek, and quickly introduced himself. Metek didn't look anything like you would expect. From his voice and attitude while on the air, you would think he was a huge man, like a football player ready to back up anything foolish he says with some muscle behind it. But instead, he was short, skinny, and looked more like a book worm than a football player. The two showmen shook hands and looked around at what Megaton has prompted. Both of them knew that all the talk and insults were just to create attention for this day.

"No hard feelings?" Metek asked.

"It's just show biz!" Big Rodger replied. They both smiled.

At that moment, the lead singer and drummer of United Corn showed up. The drummer had a lot to set up, and the singer wanted a soundcheck. They introduced themselves and asked Metek to play their music on the air. Being a newcomer to the area, Metek had not heard their music yet.

"I'll listen to it today. If I like it, I'll play it," Metek told the band members.

Big Rodger went to join his family while Metek went to get his remote set up. The two members of United Corn set out to begin their own preparation.

Cora was up early and got Megaton ready for the big show. She buffed his hoofs and hosed him down. Ben pulled the trailer up to the barn. Everything was prepared as soon as Megaton was in the trailer. Ben saw Cora was nervous.

"It's going to be great," Ben said. "You're ready. Megaton is ready. Just consider it another day of practice."

"I know Megaton can do it. I'm worried about my part," she answered. "What if I make a mistake? Megaton will look bad, and everyone will think Megaton let down the whole town. Why did I ever agree to this?"

"Come here," Ben said and sat on the fender of the horse trailer. Cora sat next to him. "I think you got that attitude from my side of the family. 'Don't take chances, stick with what's safe.' Now your mom, that's another story. She was bold, and she wasn't afraid to try things. She wasn't a showoff, but she wasn't timid either. You know, you're a lot like her. You have that ability in you too. When you get into that arena, it will be you and Megaton. Forget about everything else. It will be just the two of you, and Megaton will do anything for you."

Cora felt better after hearing Ben's supportive words. The arena and the contest didn't seem so scary now. She felt a new kind of confidence, hearing she was a lot like her mother. Like a flash, she started to remember all the things that the two of them had done together, and for the first time, she saw in her mind's eye her mothers' confidence.

Megaton was quickly led into the horse trailer, and Cora jumped into the truck. Ben drove up to the house to pick up Aunt Vivian. The Scarecrow fest was one of the few times Vivian went into town. Soon, the four of them were on their way off the farm and down the road.

It was just before ten-thirty when the La Beau truck pulled up to Wadlow Park. They were told by one of Cora's classmates who was working in the parking lot to park up on the north side of the arena in a spot reserved just for them. Cora's classmate informed them a place on the South end was reserved for the other horse but had not shown up yet.

"What if he doesn't show?" Cora asked.

"Then I guess we'll just put on our own show just like we've been doing every day for the past few weeks on our farm. We'll show everyone what they want to see. We'll show them what Megaton is capable of," Ben answered. Big Rodger soon walked up to the truck and greeted them.

"Hey, Ben, Hey, Cora. Hello Vivian. Megaton ready? You guys are early," he said.

"We want to walk Vivian around to see the scarecrows before the show," Ben told him.

"There are some outstanding ones this year." Big Rodger told Vivian, who smiled. "Okay, Cora. The plan is that United Corn will play. Then they will play the 'Megaton Song,' and you bring in Megaton."

"Do I ride or lead him?" Cora asked.

"Hmm... It's up to you. Whatever makes you comfortable. I have a lot I have to get to, so I'm going to run," Big Rodger told them and went off to set up the live feed of Metek's radio show.

Megaton was backed out of the La Beau trailer and hitched to a steel ring. The three La Beaus walked towards the shops. They passed the bleachers of the arena where many people had already shown up to stake out their spots. Cheers and well wishes came showering down from some of the early arrivals. One thing that Cora didn't expect were the boos, hisses, and catcalls from the fans of the other horse sitting in the same bleachers.

"Ignore them." Ben coached.

"Ignore what?" she joked, and nervously laughed.

"There's your mom," Ben said, looking at her and winked.

Scarecrows lined both sides of the streets like an honor guard for two solid blocks. Aunt Vivian was all smiles as they approached them. She didn't understand the puns of the scarecrow names, but it didn't matter. You didn't need to understand the humor to enjoy them.

Halfway down the first block, in front of the barbershop, they met Dr. Bodie and his wife Ann, who were walking in the other direction. They all exchanged greetings, and Dr. Bodie assured Cora that he would be there to see all the action.

"Tell us about the other horse," implored Ben.

"I really don't know anything. I'm not his vet. I can tell you this, Cora. I know Megaton will put his whole heart and every muscle into whatever you want him to do."

"Can he get hurt?" Cora asked.

"I don't think so. What was set up sounds safe to me." Dr. Bodie assured her.

"We have reserved seats. Come and sit with us." Ben invited.

"That sounds good," said Ann Bodie. "We'll join you in a bit. Oh, Vivian, look at the scarecrow in front of Wally's Leather shop. I think you'll like it." And with that, the Bodie's went on their way.

Wally Carlson was the leather maker that made Megaton's custom saddle. He did repair work and made custom goods. He made the cowboy boots that the singer of United Corn was wearing. The anti-smoking scarecrow in front of his shop had a good chance of winning that year. It was a medium-size mannequin about the size of a teenager. It had sneakers, jeans, and a sweatshirt like many teenagers wore with a pumpkin head and cigarette butts for teeth. The chest was cut away, and inside the chest cavity were two large sponges as lungs with melted road tar painted on them. The name of the anti-smoking scarecrow was Nick O' Teen.

When the La Beau trio walked up to the scarecrow in front of Wally Carlson's store, Ben smiled after reading the name. A look of disgust washed over both Cora and Vivian's faces at the same time. It was a compelling visual message. Ben stepped into Wally's shop, along with Cora and Vivian, who wanted to avoid staring at the scarecrow any longer than necessary.

"That's quite a scarecrow you've got out front," Ben said.

"It is indeed. Warren Lind made it. Do you know him, Cora? He's about your age, I think." Wally replied as he turned to Cora.

Cora and Warren took the bus together. Warren's father had died from lung cancer after years of smoking.

"I know him. We call him Skipper. We see each other on the bus and in a couple of classes at school," answered Cora. "He always coming up with puns."

"How's Megaton's saddle and pulling gear holding up?" Wally asked.

"It's fine, even with all the use we've been giving it lately," Cora replied. Ben jumped in and told them they needed to move along if they wanted to see more scarecrows before the show.

"I'm closing up my shop for the contest and so are a lot of the other shops. We all want to watch Megaton in action," Wally informed them. "Good luck to Megaton," he shouted to them as they left his shop.

Cora and Aunt Vivian walked back to the horse trailer together after looking at the rest of the scarecrows. Ben took some extra time in town. He needed to go to the hardware store for some supplies he needed back on the farm before it closed down for the show. When Cora and Aunt Vivian got close to the bandshell, they could hear the master of ceremonies Big Rodger Staley. He had a cardboard box on his hand with a face on it and a mouth that opened and closed. He was doing his ventriloquist routine. Unlike most ventriloquist acts, Rodger was the funny one delivering the punch lines of the jokes. The puppet, which Big Roger named Block Head, was the straight man setting up the jokes.

"What kind of work do you do?" the puppet asked Big Roger, who barely moved his lips.

"I'm the world's greatest lumberjack. I can chop a tree down in no time. Any tree, anywhere." Big Roger answered the puppet setting up the next exchange of the act.

"Where did you work?"

"Have you ever heard of the Sahara Forest?"

"You mean the Sahara Desert."

"It is now." Big Roger answered as he kicked his leg in the air to emphasize the punch line. The crowd responded with a mix of groans and chuckles, which Big Roger didn't mind. It meant they were at least paying attention. He wanted to get the crowd excited and getting them engaged one way or another was more important than just getting a laugh. After a few more jokes, he and Block Head began interviewing the members of United Corn.

"I hear you have a new song for Megaton. What other songs have you got for us?" Big Roger asked.

"I'm writing a song about chickpeas. I don't have words yet, so I'll just hummus the tune." The singer said, soliciting more groans from the audience. Jokes like that continued on for a few minutes.

Back at the La Beau trailer, two teenaged boys walked up and introduced themselves as fans of Jumbo Jim and started to trash talk.

"Megaton is so stupid, his brain is the size of a golf ball," one called out.

Cora paid no attention to the remark that she judged as a lame insult, not even well thought out.

"Megaton is so ugly, he should only be allowed to go out at night."

Cora didn't like that put down.

"Go away. You have no business here." Cora commanded.

"It's a free country," the bullies told her.

"You have no business here. Go away!" Cora repeated.

43

"Yeah. Go away!" Vivian said.

As soon as the boys heard Vivian speak, they sensed a new opportunity to be exceptionally cruel. Like a wolf spying an injured lamb, their focus shifted onto a newly found, even more vulnerable target.

"Hey retard, do you even know what we're talking about?" taunted the taller boy. Cora flashed with and anger and defended Vivian.

"She's not retarded!" snapped Cora.

"You see big horsey today?" the smaller of the boys asked Vivian mockingly slow.

"Don't talk to her like that! Don't even talk to her at all. Leave us alone!" Megaton heard the tone of Cora's voice and sensed she needed help. Cora and Vivian tried to walk away, but the two bullies kept moving, stepping side-to-side into their path.

"Let us go," Cora demanded.

"We're not stopping you," the taller boy said. Cora was angry now. She pushed the smaller boy to the side so they could walk past. This time the taller one didn't stand in their way. But as Cora walked past him, he put his hands on her shoulders from behind and held her back.

"Keep your hands off me," Cora yelled.

Megaton, tied to the trailer, heard the yell. Sensing the desperation in her voice, he was determined to help her. He pulled back, rocking the horse trailer back and forth. The reins broke, and he was free to run to help his friend. Megaton ran right up to them, reared up with anger, and stood between them and the bullies. He snorted, shook his head, and stomped his white hoof on the ground as if to say, "No more."

The boys took one looked at Megaton and froze in their tracks. Megaton walked up to them and knocked both bullies to the ground with one push of his head. When they were able to get themselves back up, they ran away as fast as they could.

"Megaton! How did you get here? You were tied up!" Cora asked out loud. Cora immediately noticed the broken reins. "We're going to need the reins for the obstacle course."

Cora took the broken reins, and the three of them went to the trailer. There were no extra reins.

"What do we do now? There's no time to go back to the farm, and Wally's is closed. Maybe I can tie the pieces together," she thought.

The leather was cut too thick and wide to be any good at tying together. As it turned out, the knot was much too big, making the reins too short. Cora would have to lean forward and reach out too far to make them work.

The interview with the band ended, and the jokes stopped. Big Rodger left the bandshell, and United Corn began their set, which would include the song they wrote for Megaton.

Ben came sauntering up to the trailer from the hardware store and seeing Cora, Vivian, and Megaton knew right away, something was wrong.

"What happened?" he asked.

"The reins are broken, and now they're too short," Cora answered. She proceeded to tell Ben the whole story of the boys, Vivian and what Megaton did.

"Who are they? Where are they?" Ben demanded.

"Don't worry about those stupid boys. They both ran off," Cora told him.

"When this is all over, we'll look for them. Now let's look in the truck and see if we can rig up something for reins," Ben told her.

They searched high and low, but nothing they found

would work. United Corn was on their second song, and time was running out.

"Dad, Megaton and I can do it. We'll just use voice commands. I'm sure we can do it." Cora insisted.

"You know, Cora, I do believe the two of you can," Ben responded.

United Corn finished their second song when Ben came up with the idea to make one rain out of the two broken ones without using a knot. He took his pocket knife and cut a slit in each leather strap. He then ran one through the other at the slot joining the two together to make one long strap.

"This should help in the obstacle course," he said. Cora climbed up onto Megaton and sat in the saddle. She took the one rein and started to teach Megaton what to do with just one rein to work with. She pulled back on the rein, and Megaton stopped. Just as if he had two reins working. Cora was pleased with his performance. She then got him to go in any direction by voice commands.

"Dad, I think this is going to work," she yelled with excitement. She decided to ride into the arena. She rode Megaton up to the entrance and waited for their cue to enter.

Ben and Vivian headed for their reserved seats. Big Rodger told the handlers of Jumbo Jim to enter the arena immediately after the end of the fourth song. He conveniently left out the fact that the fifth song was going to be Megaton's theme. Big Roger planned to have the other horse enter and wait in place while Megaton entered in a grand entrance.

As instructed, the other horse walked into the arena on cue while Megaton stood still waiting. United Corn talked to the crowd for a minute, further diluting the emphases of

Jumbo Jim's entrance. On Big Roger's nod, the lead singer of United Corn called out.

"Ladies and Gentlemen, your hometown hero... Megaton!" The guitar player strummed a hard C chord, and the Megaton song began blasting from the P.A. system. The tune was immediately recognizable by everyone to the crowd as America the Beautiful. When the singer of United Corn started to sing the words, many in the crowd instinctively stood up and turned their heads towards Megaton's entrance. Big Roger smiled at the scene he had produced. It was full of drama and excitement. No matter which horse ended up winning, Big Roger had put on a show.

> *Oh, powerful and full of pride, a stallion full of might.*
> *A big and gentle giant stands a true majestic sight.*
> *Oh, Megaton, Oh Megaton, our town's pride stands*
> *with thee.*
> *So do your best. You'll pass the test.*
> *A champion you'll be.*

As the song played, Megaton and Cora entered the arena under thunderous applause. Big Rodger asked the band about the Megaton song.

"Isn't that the tune to America the Beautiful?"

"Yeah, we borrowed it from one of the eight verses. You know that song has eight verses?" He lorded his music knowledge over Rodger.

"There are verses no one ever uses like 'Oh beautiful for pilgrim feet, whose stern impassioned stress, a thoroughfare of freedom beat, across the wilderness.' Those verses... no one ever uses them," the drummer said.

Both horses were in the arena now, no more than fifteen feet apart. The crowd looked in awe at the two giants. Six thousand pounds of muscle stood before their eyes. Big Rodger, without his puppet, stood on stage and picked up the microphone to address the crowd.

"Welcome to Wadlow Park. What a beautiful day! Are you ready for the challenge?" Big Roger asked the crowd.

"I said, 'Are you ready for the challenge?'" Big Roger repeated whipping up the crowd for a more enthusiastic response.

"Here is what we have for you. Three challenges, each worth points to be judged and awarded by our distinguished judges. Our judges are Tina Talbet from Curl Up and Dye Hair Salon, Men and women's styling at 513 Bow Street. Randy Philips from Philip's Muffler, 878 Hunter Drive. He does brakes too, people. And George Geege from, Geege's Nursery, 1096 Shoe Factory Road. George has hundreds of plants, annuals, and perennials. Let's hear it for our judges. Show your appreciation, and please visit their stores for all of your hairstyling, tune-up, and gardening needs!" The crowd complied with a round of obligatory applause.

"First up," Big Roger announced, "we will have a display of Voice commands. Next will be the obstacle course. Then finally, the dead weight pull. No partial points will be given for the dead weight pull. Its winner takes all for the last event, folks. Handlers, are you ready? Spectators, are you ready?"

Big Rodger raised the microphone up to his mouth in one hand and lifted his other hand high over his head in a grand gesture to get things started.

"Handlers, are you ready? Judges, are you ready? Go!" he yelled. The two horses both started, then stopped at the same time. Then started at the same time again then stopped again. In a lurching motion, like two people trying to pass each other in a narrow hallway, neither knew who was to go first. The crowd went wild with laughter. With all his preparations and careful checking, Big Rodger forgot to set up just who was to go first. Thinking quickly, Cora called out to Big Rodger.

"We'll let our guests go first." She wasn't merely being polite or hospitable. She wanted time for Megaton to get used to the arena and the sound of the crowd.

Metek reported, "Jumbo Jim is going first, and from the looks of it, Megaton is in no hurry to get beat."

The handler held the reins of the other horse and started to give his voice commands. Jumbo Jim was unsure and slow to respond. It was clear that voice commands were not a good fit for him. The judges took note.

Soon it was Megaton's turn. The crowd grew quiet. Cora let go of the one rein, stood in front of him, and said, "Megaton." She stepped back. Megaton stepped forward. She called, and Megaton followed her lead. "HEE," she called. Megaton moved to the right. The crowd cheered and clapped. "HAW," Megaton went to the left. The judges took note of what they saw.

"That's the end of the voice command part. Let's hear it for our contestants," Big Rodger announced to the crowd as Metek passed on the news to the radio listeners.

"If only you could see what just happened. These horses are unbelievable!"

United Corn played another song in between the events. Metek repeated the agenda, voiced through a short advertisement, and then began to describe what the arena looked like for those listening on the radio.

"This is a fine obstacle course today," Metek described. "It starts with a gate the riders will ride up to, open, ride through, and then close behind them. Next, the team must weave through five barrels and traverse a field of tires on the ground, which then leads to a split rail fence. Here the horses must make right and left turns. Finely a ride back to the gate that the riders must once more open, ride through, and close."

Cora became worried. With only one rein to direct Megaton through the maze of challenges, her confidence was wavering. Just a moment later, Big Rodger spoke up and said to the crowd, "We have it all planned out this time, folks. Megaton will have the honors of going first."

In addition to voice commands, horses can be heel trained and learn to respond to go left or right as their riders push their heels against the horse's flanks or sides. With Megaton's width and custom saddle, Cora had never taught him that system. As she approached the gate, she now wished she had.

Cora sat up straight in the custom saddle and thought she'd teach him now. They rode up next to the gate. Cora reached out, unhooked the latch swung the gate open, and rode through. Now they had to get back and close the gate. Cora planned to ride in a big circle just to keep going to the left until Megaton was back at the gate. She flipped the rein over Megaton's head to his left side, and with her left foot, kept tapping Megaton. This worked out just fine, and soon Cora closed the gate. The barrels were next. This time she used voice commands. She tapped on the right side of Megaton's neck with her hand as she yelled, "HEE" as they cleared the first barrel. The call of "Haw" coincided with taps on the left side of his neck, and they rounded the second barrel. This was how they made it through all of them, not touching one.

Metek could hardly talk from laughing so hard. He tried reporting the hees and haws over the radio and didn't know quite how to describe it. The crowd loved it, and the judges were very impressed.

Megaton walked up to the field of tires. Knowing horses don't like to walk on uneven ground, Big Roger thought this tricky addition to the obstacle course would be a crowd-pleaser. Cora coaxed him with her heels. He slowly walked forward, stepping in some tires and on some others. Teetering on the uneven surface made Megaton nervous, and Cora could feel it.

"Come on, Megaton, you can do this," she said calmly to reassure him. He heard her soothing voice. Knowing this is what Cora wanted gave him the courage to tromp on forward. A few more steps and soon, the patch of tires was behind them.

By the time Megaton reached the maze of the split-rail fence, he had quickly learned the tapping method Cora was constantly reinforcing since the beginning of the obstacle course. Cora felt her horse's confidence, and looking out at the crowd, she thought about her mother and what Ben had said about her being a lot like her. She dropped the one rein and put both hands up in the air giving the crowd a show. Megaton walked through the fence maze with very little help from Cora besides the light taps she gave with her heels. The crowd was in awe of what they saw. Ben was also thinking of Elsa when he turned to Vivian, Dr. Bodie, and Anne.

"That's my girl. That's my Cora," he said with a proud grin. Megaton and Cora completed the split rail fence maze and headed back to the gate. They opened it and went through. Instead of making a wide circle, Cora just pushed her heel hard into Megaton's side, who turned around in place. She closed the gate behind her, and Megaton was done with the course. The crowd exploded into cheers and applause.

Jumbo Jim went through the course without any trouble or mistakes. Jumbo Jim's rider used both reins to guide the horse as one usually would. The crowd was not overly impressed, but they did complete the course.

Metek reported that Jumbo Jim did much better than he actually did. He was more interested in creating drama and a good story than necessarily reporting the truth. He was, after all, still in Jumbo Jim's corner and said things such as "He's weaving through the barrels with the greatest of ease" and "He's stepping through the tires like a professional dancer." The few people in the crowd that had radios with them cocked their heads when they heard Metek's play-by-play clearly not match what they were seeing.

The next event was the dead weight pull. Only the judges knew the actual score at this point, and they were not saying. Everyone thought it was one-sided with Megaton way in the lead. Big Rodger was back in the bandshell with Block Head on hand filling time while the high school volunteers cleared the obstacles and prepped the arena for the final event.

Metek climbed up in the bandshell to interview Big Rodger. It was a strange and bold move for Metek to bring a ventriloquist act over the radio, but that didn't stop him from trying.

"Who do you suppose is in the lead?" Metek asked.

"I would like to know myself," added Block Head.

"The one with the most points!" answered Big Rodger supplying the punch line. More moans came from the crowd as the interview went on like that until the arena was ready for the dead weight pull.

Before the final event, however, Big Rodger has set

up one more surprise for everyone. He had the chance of working with two of the most significant horses around and wanted to satisfy a personal curiosity of his.

"What's this?" Metek asked.

"Yeah! What crazy thing are you doing now?" asked Block Head.

The volunteers brought out two U-shaped steel bars with hooks for chains.

"Oh, this?" answered Big Rodger. "You know the jeans with the picture of two horses pulling in opposite directions with the jeans in the middle?"

"Yes, I have a pair of those jeans on right now," Metek said. He didn't.

"Ok, did you hear that listeners?" Metek asked. "We are going to test the validity of the jean label live, right here on this radio program!"

"Do you think the crowd wants to see this?" asked Block Head.

"You want to see this?" Big Rodger asked the crowd. The crowd yelled back.

"What?" asked Big Rodger. "I can't hear you!"

"Yeah, Yeah, YEAH," screamed the crowd even louder this time.

"Alright. Bring out the jeans donated from Tyler's Work and Play Apparel, 9675 North Trail Road." Roger vigorously waved his arms to volunteers waiting off stage as he managed to squeeze in another commercial for a local merchant. The two giant horses were led into the center of the arena. A chain was hooked up to each horse. Then to the two upside-down U-shaped steel bars with one side of the U in each pant leg. Cora and the other handler looked at each other and went along with it. It looked just like the label on the jeans had come to life.

"I've always wanted to try this," Big Rodger whispered to Metek. Metek reported all the details.

"Horses ready?" asked Big Rodger. "On 'pull'… One… Two… Three…. Pull!" The mighty horses took two steps. The denim jeans shredded apart like a tissue paper kite in a rainstorm. The crowd laughed, yelled, and applauded.

"That's it? That's all?" Metek laughingly questioned. Everyone expected something more dramatic. They thought the jeans would hold up better.

"Are you kidding? What did you expect?" Big Rodger asked everyone in the crowd. "Look at the size of these horses," the showman in him just wanted to make the label come to life for everyone and himself to see. "Now you all can tell everyone you know you saw it live right here at Wadlow Park. How many people can say that?" Big Rodger told the crowd.

Megaton and the other horse stayed in the arena while the dead weight drag was set up. The high school volunteers set out red and white flags twenty yards apart with a yellow banner at the starting point. This was the contest the crowd had been waiting for, pure muscle power against muscle power.

The rules stated that Megaton and the Jumbo Jim would be hitched to the same sled with field stones for weight.

"Cora needs be careful with this," Dr. Bodie told Ben. "That other horse looks big and strong. If the weight is too much and it goes on too long, it can hurt Megaton's legs. It could cripple him."

"How should Cora handle it?" asked Ben.

"I think we're ahead in points. Tell her to not push Megaton too hard. Even if this event ends in a tie, this challenge won't hurt our chances of winning overall," Dr.

Bodie advised. Ben left the reserved seats, went into the arena, and walked up to Cora and Megaton.

"Dad, what's up?" Cora asked.

"Megaton will put everything he's got into this if you want him to. Don't push him too far. That other horse looks older. He may be stubborn with age, and if his handler pushes him, he just may give up."

"Thanks, Dad. I'll remember that. I'll be careful."

"I'll be sitting right over there with the Bodies." Ben pointed towards his seats in the stands.

Big Rodger, back at the microphone, yelled, "Handlers are you ready?" The two handlers nodded and waved to signal they were. Megaton was up first. Big Rodger gave the command, "GO."

The sled with the fieldstone easily slid past the flags. Jumbo Jim was now hitched up to the sled. He, too, pulled the sled seemingly without any effort at all.

Megaton was up again after more stones were added to the sled. Megaton took a big step forward, and the chain became tight. Megaton felt the weight of the additional stones.

"Pull, Megaton, pull!" Cora coached. He stepped forward. Again, the sled started moving the new weight and was not a problem once he started walking. Jumbo Jim was hitched to the vehicle, and soon it too went by the final flag.

This went on and on between the two horses for several heats. Big Rodger would call out the estimated weight of each pull. The only break the two horses had was while the other was being hitched up. It wasn't too long before the field stones were higher than the sides of the sled.

Megaton was in the middle of the 6th pull with Cora in front, leading him when he lost his footing. Megaton's back legs fell, and he landed on his knees with the strain of the sled just around the white flag. The crowd gasped at the sight. The last thing they wanted to see was either horse get hurt. Cora dropped the lead and ran to his side. Megaton got up, stood up straight, shook his head as if nothing had happened, and step after step finished the drag. The crowd went crazy with applause and cheers.

The sled was brought back, and the Jumbo Jim was hitched up. He stood straight and firm. His handler gave the lead a tug and started to take a step forward, feeling the weight of the sled. He took another step and stopped. His handler gave the lead another tug, but the horse didn't move as if to say, "I have had enough." The dead pull was over, and it was time for the judges to decide the winner.

Ben and Dr. Bodie ran to Megaton and Cora. "You did wonderfully. How are you feeling?" Ben asked.

"I'm fine," she told him. "Dr. Bodie, look at Megaton's hind legs. Is he alright?" Dr. Bodie gave Megaton a look over.

"He's not skinned up. There's no harm. Just walk him around for a few minutes," he instructed Cora. Dr. Bodie took it upon himself to go check in on the other horse as well. When he went to Jumbo Jim's trailer, he introduced himself, "I'm a veterinarian, is your vet here?" he asked the other handler.

"He is," the handler answered. The two Vets talked for a while, and Dr. Bodie looked over the other horse.

The crowd was growing impatient, waiting to hear the announcement of the winner.

"I'm sorry. I'm really am sorry the judging is taking a while." Big Roger updated the crowd. "Anyone want to hear another song from United Corn? Can we have another song?"

"Uhm, sure," the lead singer quickly decided. "The

last time we played this song was at the County Fair. Let's hope this night ends better than the last time we played it," he joked. Block Head saw an opening jumped in, "What a mess that made of the fairgrounds."

"I remember that," Big Roger said. "It reminded me of the explosion in the French cheese factory."

"Why is that?" Block Head asked.

"Da Brie was everywhere!" Big Roger eagerly answered the puppet. The entire crowd groaned in unison, and an anonymous voice from the seats called out demanding for the band to start.

Big Roger ran off the stage, leaving the band to play one last song. When it was over, Big Roger returned with the band playing, but this time as if it were meant to be only background music.

"WOW, how was that folks? Wasn't that some show?" Big Rodger asked the crowd. The crowd cheered and applauded in answer to his question.

"What a show folks, what a show for this city boy to see. I've never seen anything like it." Metek reported back to his listeners as he downplayed the part about the other horse losing the dead pull.

"Judges, do you have your results?" Big Rodger asked.

Tina was elected to be the spokesman for the judges. She was dressed nicely, and her hair was perfect. The two guys didn't wear anything special for the occasion, and both were somewhat stage shy.

"Yes, we have," Tina said as she walked up on stage and handed Big Rodger an envelope. He opened it and looked.

"Would you do the honors?" he asked Tina as he handed back the opened envelope for her to announce.

"Anything for you, Rodger. For voice commands out of a possible ten points, to Jumbo Jim, we award... eight points. For Megaton, we award... eight points." The crowd cheered. "For the obstacle course, out of a possible ten points, we award Megaton... ten points. And Jumbo Jim.... also ten points." The crowd showed their disappointment with the tie calling out some boos and hisses. "The points are tied, so by winning the dead pull, we do hereby declare Megaton the winner!"

The crowd yelled and applauded. Big Rodger let the crowd's reaction peak, and as soon as he heard it begin to dwindle, he quickly spoke into the microphone.

"That's all we have for you today. I hope you all enjoyed our show. Stop by the shops and vote for a scarecrow."

United Corn went right into the Megaton song. Some people sang along, and some started to leave their seats. The few fans of Jumbo Jim's that were in attendance booed yelled things like "foul" and "cheaters." Vivian and Anne Bodie ran down to Cora and Megaton.

"I'm so happy for both of you," Anne told them.

"I was afraid I hurt Megaton during the dead pull when Megaton lost his footing," Cora said.

"You did good. You both did good." Vivian told her.

The group headed back to the horse trailer, and moments later, Dr. Bodie caught up to them.

"Dr. Bodie, when you went to check out the other horse, is everything ok?" Cora asked.

"Yes, Cora. He's fine. He didn't hurt himself in the pull. He just didn't have the stamina or strength to work any harder," Dr. Bodie told her. "Ben, I also learned something else you might find interesting."

The whole Staily family was at the trailer to congratulate Megaton and Cora when they walked up.

"Cora, you did great. Do you know what this means?" Rose asked.

"I'm not sure what?" Cora wondered.

"You and Megaton are now true champions!" Rose told her.

"On behalf of the chamber of commerce, and the town, thank you both for a wonderful afternoon," Big Rodger gratefully told her.

"What did you want to tell me?" Ben asked Dr. Brodie.

"Jumbo Jim's handler told me he was sired by an escaped horse after the tornado. Jumbo, Jim's father, was Thor. That means Megaton and Jumbo Jim are brothers!"

everal months later, winter was nearing its end, and soon spring would take its place. Megaton and Cora took every opportunity to ski whenever snow had been on the ground. Every Saturday, they went to Wadlow Park. Cora skied all the way there being pulled by Megaton. Sometimes Sookie ran alongside too. Sookie, with his dense golden fur, loved the cold and snow. The three of them become very well known around town. Young kids brought sleds to the park, and Cora would hitch them up to Megaton for the kids to sled behind him.

On one balmy, warm Saturday, the air was heavy with moisture. The snow on the ground was three inches deep from a storm a few days earlier. Megaton and Cora were planning their trip to Wadlow Park without Sookie since Ben had taken him on an errand in his pickup truck.

Cora told Vivian of her plans to ski to Wadlow Park. She got Megaton ready for their outing by grabbing some apples and carrots. They were prepared to have some Saturday fun.

The park was packed with kids. The warn air made all the kids want to be outside after being in school all week.

The sledding hill was busy. The skating pond was almost elbow-to-elbow, and laughter filled the air.

"Megaton!" someone yelled. The word quickly spread around Wadlow Park that Megaton was arriving. Kids started lining up to get pulled around on their sleds. Cora chose the best sled of the lot and hitched it up for all of the rides. This way, even the kids who didn't bring a sled could still get a ride, and Cora didn't have to hitch and unhitch for every rider.

Megaton would walk and trot around the skating pond with one or two kids on the sled, and Cora would ride on Megatons back. Everyone would watch, and parents that were there with their children snapped pictures. Cora was delighted to offer and share this experience.

On one trip around the skating pond, Skipper Lind was waving to Cora from the skating pond. He was an excellent skater and loved playing hockey on the ice when other hockey players showed up. Cora waved back without stopping. After a few more trips around the pond, it started to snow. Small, wet, heavy flakes fell at first without anyone giving it much thought. It was just snow.

Mrs. Lind soon came to pick up Skipper and drive him home. Before leaving the park, he went over to Cora and Megaton.

"Cora, my mom heard on the radio that a big snowstorm is on the way. Maybe you should start for home. I know it takes you and Megaton a while to get home." he warned her.

"A few more rides around the pond first, and then we'll head home," she assured him. "Thanks for telling me." Cora never thought there could be any danger in snow.

"See ya Monday," Skipper said, running off to the car where his mom was waiting.

"See ya!" Cora yelled back to him.

The sky was looking very strange. While one half of the sky looked clear, the other half was dark gray, almost black. Meteorologists call this a shelf cloud. Snowflakes continued to fall. Soon the flakes started getting more substantial and massive. Megaton made his last trip around the pond, and with the final ride given, they were ready to go home.

All that was left was to return the sled they used. Cora looked for the boy from whom she borrowed it. It became hard to see through the falling snow.

"Let's look by the sledding hill," she murmured to Megaton. When they got to the hill, they found a friend of the boy.

"He went to find you!" the friend chuckled.

"We have a long way to go. Can I leave this sled with you?" she asked.

"Sure, I'll give it to him," he told her as the snow continued to get heavier. The snowstorm suddenly took an unusual turn and quite unexpectedly shot out a bolt of lightning followed quickly by a clap of rolling thunder. Cora had never heard thunder in a snowstorm before.

Ben returned from his errand and asked Vivian if Cora had returned. Vivian told him she was still out with Megaton at Wadlow Park.

"I don't like the looks of this snowstorm," Ben told Vivian, "It could get bad real soon," he said with a tone of concern.

Cora took the skis down from the saddle, stepped into them, and started skiing home. The snow fell even heavier now. It piled up fast, and in about thirty minutes, had already added two inches to the snow on the ground. It was almost impossible to see. Cora took off the skis and climbed up to the saddle. Megaton trudged through the heavy snow picking up his hoofs higher than he usually would. His head was down, and his neck parallel to the ground. With Cora on his back, they headed home.

Ben made calls to people who might have seen the two of them. He was told by one person that they had left Wadlow Park and were on their way home. Ben felt better from the news. He still worried, though, as any loving parent would.

"Vivian, would you make some fresh coffee? I'll have a cup and give them some time. Then I'll go out looking for them."

Sookie sensed something was wrong and started to pace back and forth at the door. Ben opened the door and let him out. He ran around the yard sniffing the air. He came to a specific spot and started to howl without stopping.

Cora could no longer see anything through the heavy snow. She let go of the reins and wrapped her arms around Megaton's neck; Megaton was on his own now. Cora leaned forward and hugged his neck tightly. She talked to him calmly.

"This is some snow, huh, Megaton?" She was mumbling, saying anything to keep calm and to relax Megaton. Time ticked away, and Ben was soon ready to go out to look for them. In his worried condition, Ben was losing his patients.

"Can't that dog stop howling?" he snapped. Ben yelled out the door, "Quiet!" Sookie stopped howling just a moment then started up again. He continued howling, only stopping to catch his breath.

Cora could feel how hard and tiring it was for Megaton to walk in the ever-deepening snow. Cora couldn't see where they were going and wondered if Megaton could. Her sense of direction was gone, and she couldn't see any landmarks.

"Are we lost?" she asked Megaton. "I don't even know

what direction we're going." Megaton just kept walking and walking. "Maybe we should rest under some trees for a while." She suggested to Megaton. The falling snow was so heavy, all she could see were different shades of gray. Megaton, however, just kept walking. His gate never varied. It was slow and deliberate. If they were headed in the wrong direction, he would just keep walking.

Ben put on his coat and was going to warm up the truck. Sookie was still hollering as if to provide a sound beacon for Megaton to find his way home through the heavy snow.

"Can't he be quiet? Does he have to keep howling?" he snapped. "That howling is not helping," Ben complained as his worry shortened his temper.

"Maybe it is," Vivian replied. "Maybe he's calling to them." No sooner had she said it the howling stopped. Sookie's howl changed to a bark as if someone was coming up the driveway. Ben and Vivian walked outside to see if they were home. They didn't see anyone. Sookie stopped barking and was nowhere in sight.

Megaton had walked right into the barn out of the snow and into familiar surroundings. It felt warm and safe. Sookie soon entered the barn on his own. Cora slid down from the saddle and opened the stall gate for Megaton. Together they walked in. Megaton was very tired, but more than that, he was dazed and dizzy. He fell to his knees and flopped on to his side.

"Megaton!" Cora screamed. "Dad. Dad!" she screamed as she ran to the house. Ben and Vivian heard Cora's cry and ran to the barn.

"It's Megaton. Hurry." Cora pleaded. "He's in the barn. He collapsed."

"I'm so glad you're alright," Ben said as he hugged her. "I was so worried!"

"Dad, I'm alright. Look at Megaton! What about Megaton? Help him, Dad, help him. Call Dr. Bodie. Call him now," she pleaded. Growing up on a farm, Ben did know a little about emergency animal care. He knelt and put his ear to Megaton's chest.

"Stay here, I'm going to call Dr. Bodie right now," he said sadly. He didn't say anything else. Cora wrapped her arms around Megaton's neck, snuggled up to him, and stroked his head.

"Rest now, just rest," she told him as she fell asleep from exhaustion. Vivian stayed in the barn sitting in a rocking chair while Cora slept. The cat paced back and forth on the railing of the stall. He knew something was wrong. Vivian got up and laid a horse blanket over Cora, not disturbing her sleep. With the blanket covering Cora, Vivian knew she was all right in the barn and returned to the house.

"Hello, Anne. Ben La Beau here. I need to talk to Otto."

Soon Dr. Bodie got on the phone, and Ben told him the whole story.

"I'm buried in snow here, Ben. But I'll get there as soon as I can. Until then, keep him warm and don't let him run around," he instructed Ben. Ben hung up the phone and updated Vivian.

"He's going to get here as soon as he can," he told Vivian. "Is Cora still with Megaton?"

"She's asleep in the barn with him," she answered. "Should we bring her in?" Vivian asked.

"No. Cora won't leave Megaton. So we may as well let her get some rest even if it's in the barn." Ben answered.

In the morning, Ben and Vivian went out to the barn to look in on Cora. With the help of a four-wheel-drive Jeep to get through the heavy snow, Dr. Bodie drove up and walked into the barn. Ben woke Cora and told her to go into the house, so Dr. Bodie could do his job.

"What's going on with Megaton?" Cora demanded.

"Wait in the house, please," Dr. Bodie asked politely. Cora strolled to the house with Ben and Vivian following. The three La Beau's sat at the kitchen table and had a hot drink. Cora didn't feel like talking. She took her hot chocolate and went to sit by the fire while Ben and Vivian stayed at the table.

"How did you know Sookie was calling to them?" Ben asked Vivian.

"I would call out to my friends if they were lost," she answered. Vivian sometimes amazed people with her insights.

"Is Megaton going to be alright?" Vivian asked.

"I don't know. I've never seen this kind of thing before. He's a strong horse. I hope he will get through this." Ben told her. He continued, "Do remember when Grandpa Claude's horse, that old broodmare Daphne, came up to the house and died on the porch? She was so big and fat we had to get the tractor and a tow truck to get her down off the porch." Ben recalled.

"I remember that. It was sad at the time, but now we laugh about it," Vivian added.

"Is Megaton dying?" Cora chimed in from the other room. Ben looked towards her and stirred his coffee.

"No, no. I don't know why I brought that up," Ben said. He couldn't help but think about what if, and what would Cora do if he did. He worried about Cora if she had to bear another loss, and his thoughts went back to Elsa.

Ben's concern was interrupted by the phone ringing. Ben got up and answered it. It was Rose Staily. She heard the talk around town that the La Beaus were looking for

Cora out in the snowstorm. Rose and Big Roger wanted to know if Cora got home all right.

"She made it home and is resting safely by the fire, Rose. Megaton, however, is not so good. He collapsed, and we don't know why. Dr. Bodie is looking at him now." Ben informed her.

"Oh, no. Do we know what's wrong?"

"Not yet," Ben told her.

"I hope he'll be all right. Tell Cora I called and let us know if you need any help with anything. We'll keep good thoughts."

"Thanks, Rose," Ben said as they said their goodbye's and hung up the phone.

Dr. Bodie came up to the porch and stomped his feet to knock the snow off. It was also his way of knocking. Cora jumped up and ran to the door.

"Is Megaton all right?" she pleaded as she opened the door.

"I'm not going to lie to you, Cora," he told her directly. "He is in danger. He's severely dehydrated, which is why he collapsed. He needs electrolytes. It's a miracle that he got you home."

"I did this him. I kept him out too long," Cora cried and broke into tears. Ben put his arm around her shoulders.

"Sweetheart, you didn't do it." Ben tried to comfort her. "You and Megaton went out for the day. That's all. Don't feel or think you did it. No one did anything."

"I drove him too hard. We stayed too long. I did this. I did this to him." Cora insisted through her tears.

"I gave him a supplement." Dr. Bodie spoke. "It's a start. We'll be able to tell more in twenty-four hours." Dr. Bodie looked Cora straight in the eye and put his hand on her shoulder. "Keep an eye on him and call me right away if anything changes. I'll come by tomorrow. He may need an intravenous transfusion."

"I'm going to stay with him," she said.

"Don't get him excited. He needs to drink and rest. Look in on him from time to time, but don't get him excited," he repeated.

The phone began to ring once again, and Vivian called out, "I'll get it." This time it was Reverend Fisher who also heard out about Cora and called worried.

"No, let me," Cora asked her aunt. Vivian handed Cora the phone. "Hello?"

"Hello. This is Reverend Fisher. Is everything okay out by you?" he asked.

"Megaton is sick. Dr. Bodie says he's dehydrated," Cora reported to him. "It's my fault. I took him out and didn't give him enough to drink. He carried me all the way home. He was hot and sweaty, carrying me through the heavy, wet snow with nothing to drink. I'm a terrible person. I did this to him."

"Cora, you're not a terrible person. I don't think Megaton would blame you. Do you? That horse loves you. All Megaton wanted was to get you home safe. Dr. Bodie is a fine vet, and with him in your corner and our prayers, I believe Megaton will be healthy in no time. You must believe it too." Dr. Fischer assured her. Cora heard what he said and tried to take it in. Dr. Fischer continued with his captive audience, "We'll talk more tomorrow. I'll come by and see how things are going."

Cora did feel better after that phone call. The reality of it all didn't seem so threatening anymore. She reminded herself that Megaton was back home now and was being treated by an excellent doctor. She felt better but continued to worry.

Through the evening, the three La Beau's sat in the barn, sometimes together and sometimes in pairs. Megaton didn't move at all. Each of the family members would take turns returning to the house for a while. Later in the night, Vivian was first to go to bed. Ben went a little later, and Cora was the last to leave Megaton. She felt he was strong enough to rest by himself, so she went off to bed.

Early the next morning, everyone at the La Beau house woke to the sound of Sookie's barking and many cars approaching the farm. Dr. Bodie's car was among them. He wanted to get there early with more electrolytes. He carried an intravenous bottle of electrolytes with him and hoped he wouldn't need to use it. Cora and Vivian looked out the window as Ben went to the door to greet everyone. He opened the door and looked.

"A lot of people are here. Go put on some coffee, Vivian!" he shouted. It seemed everyone from town was there.

"No need to do that, Vivian. We brought coffee and breakfast. There's some lunch and dinner, too," Peggy Dial called out as she approached the porch. Everyone that came wanted to help. Everyone brought something so the La Beau's could concentrate on getting the town hero healthy.

Dr. Bodie, on his way to the barn, passed by Reverend Fischer.

"Sometimes prayers need some science help," Dr. Bodie quipped.

"Megaton has our prayers. So you get the science part going, Dr." Reverend Fisher answered. Dr. Bodie walked into the barn. Cora expected, along with everyone else, that Dr. Bodie would come right out and say Megaton was fine. That didn't happen. He didn't come right out. He didn't come out for a very long time.

Skipper and Mrs. Lind pulled up to the house with their car radio tuned to Metek In the Morning.

"I'm deeply saddened this morning." Metek's voice poured out of the speakers. I got a call that Megaton is ill. I don't know why. I, for one, wish him a speedy recovery. I just want to add that the challenge we put together last fall was the high point of my broadcasting career. I'll never forget it and if you can hear me, 'Thank you. Megaton, get well soon.'" Skipper ran to tell Cora what Metek said.

"Cora, did you hear Metek?" Skipper cried out. "He was just talking about Megaton. He wished him well and hopes he gets well soon."

"Why isn't Dr. Bodie out yet? What could be wrong?" Cora asked Skipper.

"I don't know, Cora," he answered, shaking his head.

Rose Staily walked up to Cora and hugged her. "He'll be just fine, Cora. He's strong, and I'm sure he'll be just fine. You'll be riding and skiing in no time. Just you watch." Rose assured her.

"Then why isn't Dr. Bodie coming out? What's taking so long? I'm worried now," Cora confessed.

"I wish I had an answer for you. For now, let's just give them the time they need," then Rose changed the subject. "Cora, are you going to introduce me to your boyfriend?" Rose asked to get Cora's mind off of Megaton. Cora got all flushed.

"He's not my boyfriend! Yes, he's a friend. Yes, he's a boy," Cora responded.

"If he's a boy and a friend, doesn't that make him a boyfriend?" Rose reminded her.

"Yeah, but not a boyfriend. We go to school together. That's all," Cora insisted. "His name is Warren Lind. We call him Skipper. Rose, meet Skipper. Skipper, meet Rose

Staily," Cora replied with a snip, not liking to be teased about boyfriends. Rose's plan worked. She kept asking questions of Cora and Skipper passing time and taking Cora's mind off Megaton. Soon, Ben came out of the house and headed towards the barn.

"Wait up, Ben," Reverend Fischer called. "We'll walk together." Ben stopped, and they shook hands in front of the barn. Cora ran to catch up to them.

"Stay here, Sweetheart," Ben told her.

"Dad, I want to go in. Megaton is my horse. I can't wait any longer. Dad, don't keep me out of this," she pleaded. Ben looked at Reverend Fischer for a clue as to what to do. Ben spoke softly.

"What if it's not good? Are you ready for what you might see in there?" Ben gently asked her.

"Dad, Megaton is not just my horse. He's my link to life."

Ben looked at Cora. "Where have the years gone? You are so grown up. How did I miss that? You're a young lady now. So much like your mother." Ben looked at her and remembered the first time he laid eyes on Elsa at the auction.

"Come on, Cora, we'll face this as a family," Ben said.

"You want me with you?" Reverend Dr. Fischer asked. Ben looked at Cora. Cora looked at Ben.

"That's your call. You're welcome to come with us," Cora told him. "But my dad and I are going in together."

"I understand," he responded. "I'll be close by if you need me."

The two La Beaus got to the door of the barn. Cora slowed her pace and took Ben's hand.

"Dr. Bodie?" Cora called out.

"Come on in, Cora, someone here misses you." Dr. Bodie called back. Cora and Ben walked up to Megaton's stall. He stood tall and steady and looked much more alert. Dr. Bodie was preparing to take out an intravenous needle. "I'm just about finished," he called out as he described what was about to happen. "I'm about to take out this needle and disconnect this tube. A quick wipe over the puncture wound with this alcohol wipe, and we'll be finished. Megaton will be just fine."

Megaton walked up to the stall gate. Cora hugged her horse around his neck.

"I'm so glad you're alright," she said to Megaton. "He's alright, isn't he, Dr. Bodie?" Cora asked.

"He'll be just fine. Keep extra water around for the next few days and just keep him in the stall. Don't do anything that will make him thirsty. No long rides," the doctor ordered.

"Can I walk him out to show everyone that's he's okay?" Cora asked.

"I think so. But don't make it a long walk," Dr. Bodie answered.

Cora put the bridle on Megaton. They headed for the door.

"Cora!" Ben called out stopping her. "To think when he was born, I thought this half breed would have no place around this farm. Yet you two have won the hearts of everyone that you meet," Ben confessed.

"Come on, Megaton," Cora said. "You'll be surprised to see how many people love you."

They walked out of the barn together.

Printed in the United States
By Bookmasters